AELUMINARS
THE CHRONICLES OF BELANOR

YASHAR ZANDIE ALPINAK "ARSHAM"

Copyright © 2023 Yashar Zandie Alpinak

Aeluminars
From the Chronicles of Belanor Series Author: Yashar Zandie Alpinak "Arsham"
Copyright © 2023 by Yashar Zandie Alpinak "Arsham" All rights reserved.
No part of this book may be reproduced, stored, or transmitted in any form or by any means, electronic, mechanical, photocopying, recording, scanning, or otherwise, without written permission from the author. It is illegal to copy this book, post it anywhere on the internet, or distribute it by any other means without permission.
This novel is entirely a work of fiction. The names, characters, and incidents are all the author's imagination.
Any resemblance to actual persons, living or deceased, or incidents is completely coincidental.
Yashar Zandie Alpinak "Arsham" asserts the moral right to be identified as the author of this book.

TABLE OF CONTENTS

ACKNOWLEDGMENT

Barduk Forest

Aeluminars

Shajar'anak

Aland

Army of scrawny men

Raionar

Shajar'atash

Aramashasb

Book Credits

ACKNOWLEDGMENT

I must start by thanking my wonderful wife, Sonia. From pushing me to bring my scattered thoughts onto the paper, to reading my drafts, encouraging me to continue, and giving me thoughtful advice. I want you to know that if it weren't for you, I wouldn't even think about writing a book.

Secondly, I want to thank my parents. No matter how far away you are, you are always in my heart.

And lastly, I want to express my gratitude to all the readers who took the time to read my book.

THE CHRONICLES OF BELANOR

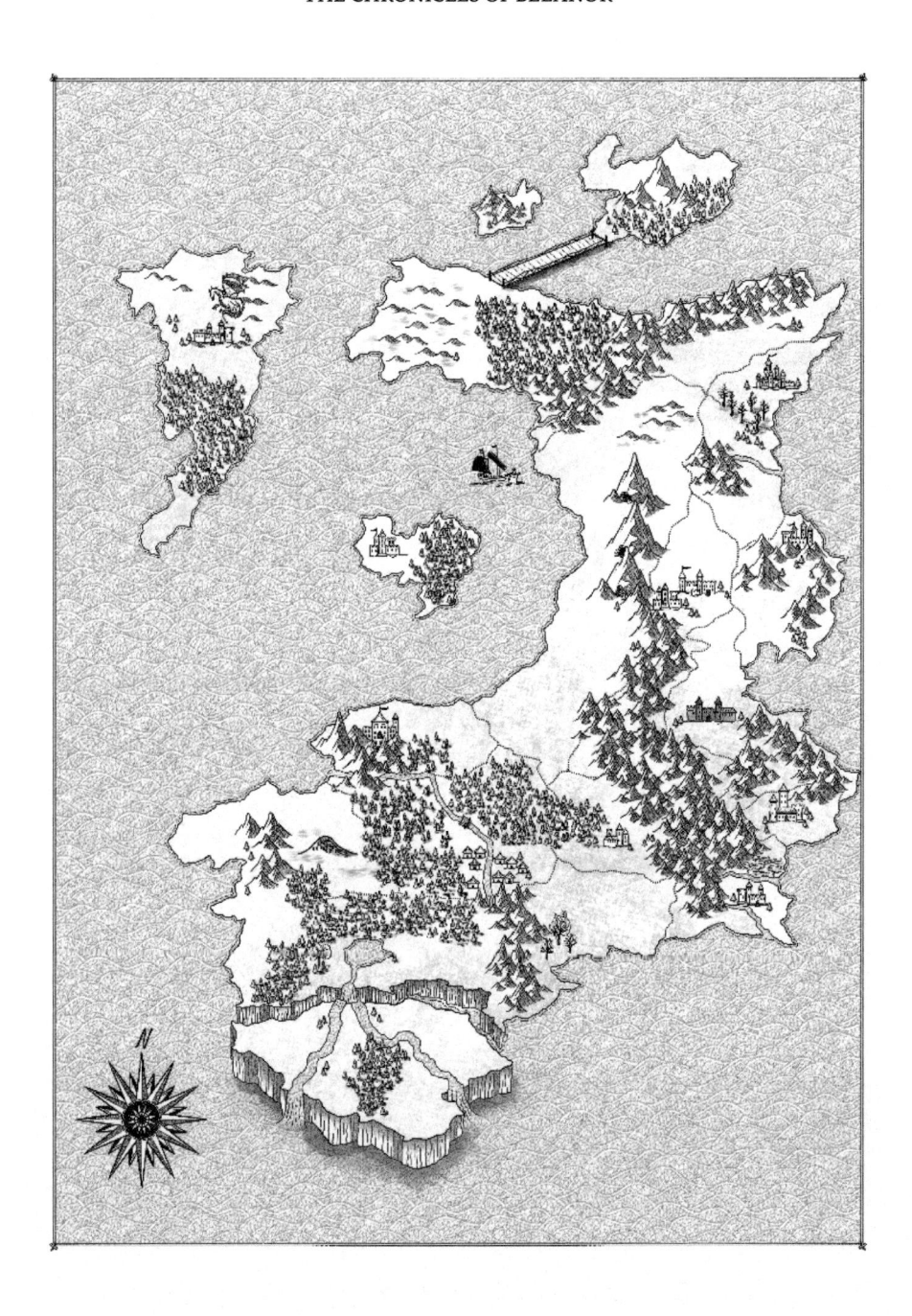

BARDUK FOREST

Scarlet opened her eyes. She found herself trapped inside something. She could not move her body but could see a dim light emanating from a tiny hole where she was trapped. She started panicking and desperately tried to get air into her lungs. In fear, she tried to push against the walls surrounding her, and with a little effort, she managed to break through and get out of what she was trapped in.

She kneeled and eagerly inhaled the air into her lungs. After coming back to her senses, she turned around and saw it was a tree where she was trapped—something like a pine but half the size and with a bigger trunk. The tree's withered and brittle trunk contrasted with its green branches, which were covered with blooming flowers.

It was dark everywhere. She started looking around; it was a forest full of trees and greenery. Even though she couldn't see the moon or sun, she could still see around her. An unknown light source illuminated the surroundings. On the ground covered with green grass, she found a pair of clothes and put them on immediately. A buttonless shirt and pants made of brown cotton fabric.

She then put on the shoes, which were made of felt and leather. There was a woven satchel and a leather scabbard belt, which she also wore.

Twenty-seven-year-old Scarlet had black-coloured hair that reached her back. She was about 165cm tall. Her slim build contributed to her attractiveness, which was already indescribable. She had bigger ears than usual, but they fit her face perfectly. She had a large birthmark on her left cheek, further emphasising her unique beauty.

Scarlet was scared, lost, and confused. She whispered, "Where am I? Is it a dream? Am I dead? Is this hell?"

"This is neither hell nor a dream," Branabus replied loudly and clearly.

Scarlet turned around to see the person who spoke to her. She saw something that she had never seen before. A pale creature with a long face, leather-like skin, and three eyes on each side of his face. He had no nose. His ears were like two holes, and he had no lips. He had no legs, or at least they weren't visible, and instead, he was floating in the air. He was dressed in a black cloak with golden embroidery in the form of tree roots. That weird-looking creature's gaze was piercing and emotionless. His hands were bony and thin.

Scarlet jumped out of fear and said, "Who the heck are you?"

"The right question is, what am I? I am what you need to start—a lead but not a leader to where and if you should reach. You are the question, and I am the answer; for a while, I believe, and about the name, my name is Branabus." He said.

Scarlet was confused and afraid. She paused for a few seconds and kept staring at Branabus.

She replied, "I don't understand. The last thing I remember is that I was hit by a car while riding my bicycle. Am I in a coma? Or… dead? What is this place?"

Branabus said, "Dead you are, and this place is called Barduk Forest. You have been resurrected to continue your journey."

"So, is this purgatory?" Scarlet sought clarification.

"Nothing like that," Branabus responded.

Scarlet did not seem to understand him. "Then what is this place?"

Branabus did not give her a specific answer. Instead, he told her, "We are in the subterranean depths of the planet where you used to live. After your death, you have been resurrected for delicate reasons. Questions are infinite, and time is short. You have a long journey ahead. We must move."

"Where are we going, then?" Scarlet was angry. She felt Branabus was taking her in rounds and rounds.

Branabus realised Scarlet was stubborn and might prove difficult to handle. He suggested, "You should meet your other fellows and begin your journey towards Melektav, your creator."

Confused, Scarlet asked, "I do not understand anything you say. Any of this doesn't make any sense." She then mumbled, "My creator?"

Scarlet noticed that on the branches of each tree, there were birds illuminating the forest with blue light. The birds had heron-like heads but were the size of swallows. Hundreds of them were there, sitting on tree branches and chanting a depressing melody. Under her feet, she could hear the rustle of orange leaves. Branabus started floating ahead and Scarlet followed him.

Branabus answered, "Nothing does until you are accustomed and keep repeating it till you become familiar with the environment. Didn't this happen in the first chapter when you were born? You cried when you saw all those faces and things around you because you didn't know them. Or when you saw me, Nours, and everything else you see here."
Branabus said this while pointing to the birds in the trees.

"So, they're called Nours," Scarlet whispered.

Scarlet followed Branabus as he began to walk through the forest. She gazed around. Green grass blanketed the forest surface. There were trees and shrubs along their path, and they could hear the soothing melody of the river in the distance.

Scarlet asked Branabus, "You said Melektav is my creator. Didn't he or she create you as well?"

"I mean what I say, and I say what I mean, Tahona. I served as the realm's guide long before Melektav was born…" Branabus replied.

Scarlet interrupted Branabus before he could finish, saying, "Wait, my name is Scarlet. Who's Tahona?"

Branabus, patient with her, said, "Scarlet was the name given to you by your Earth-bearers. I mean your parents. Every creature of Melektav and the creators before her has a name."

Scarlet, now Tahona, wondered further, "And you said this Nelektav…."

Branabus corrected her, "Melektav!"

"That's it, Melektav. She is not the only creator," Tahona said.

Branabus informed her that Melektav would be the only creator then, but her time was about to end. He added that before her, Melekahur was the sole creator.

Tahona, surprised, asked, "Is she going to die?"

"Die? No. She will fail, so this sphere will exist no more," Branabus clarified.

Tahona was taken aback. "What do you mean? Do you mean Earth? Up there? Where I was living till half an hour ago?"

Branabus confirmed her doubts. "Yes, Tahona."

Even more surprised, Tahona asked, "When?"

Branabus confirmed her doubts. "When you fail to reach Melektav."

On the left and right, Tahona observed two rivers. She continued and saw that the two rivers were approaching each other. Silver, shining and raging, yet calm and tranquil.

Tahona, with a worried tone, asked, "Do you mean everyone will die? My family? My daughter? And everything depends on me?"

"You are in plural, Tahona. You'll meet two other companions, so worry not. Your concerns for your still-living ones are venerable, though not needed. You have more serious matters that you will need to be concerned about," Branabus informed her.

Tahona wondered, "And when will these two join us, exactly? Who are they?"

Branabus shocked her when he said, "One is already here."

After walking for a few hours, at the confluence of two rivers, which flow into a waterfall, Branabus came to a stop. A shadow was getting closer to them.

AELUMINARS

Jacob stepped outside the brittle tree and knelt on the ground. He was standing naked in front of the trees, and his eyes were mesmerised by the beauty of Nours. He was a tall, slim young man of African descent. His curly hair was long, untidy, and greasy, and his blue eyes were full of emotion. He had a small scar on his left eyebrow from his childhood.

Jacob wondered, "What was I doing inside a tree? Is this a dream?"

"That was not a tree, and you are fully awake!" Adina surprised him.

Jacob turned around and saw Adina, a magnificent creature resembling a female centaur, standing before him. She was a mix of human and gazelle. Her chest was covered with green moss. Her dazzling emerald eyes were shining like twin celestial orbs. Her beautiful golden hair covered her back and chest.
Jacob saw the brown garments on the ground and started wearing them.

He looked at Adina and said calmly, "Those birds are beautiful and... sad."

Adina, agreeing with him, said, "They are sorrowful because their cycle might be coming to an end. They are Nours, blessed birds of this realm. They have been created by Melektav, your creator, to bring light upon three Aeluminar warriors."

Jacob smirked and said, "Am I supposed to be one of these valiant warriors? You picked the wrong guy... what is your name?"

"I am Adina, your guide, chosen by Mawu during your journey, dear Astiak," Adina informed him.

Jacob was growing agitated and retorted, "I told you. You're at the wrong door. I am Jacob, Jacob Abrahams."

Adina, empathetic about Jacob's ignorance, told him, "Your parents delivered you on Earth, but your real name, which was chosen by Melektav, is Astiak."

Jacob, now Astiak, wondered in confusion, "So, I am dead; I have a different name here; I am a warrior; all this and... you! It's just a lot to digest. I mean no offence, but I haven't seen anything like you."

"Take your time, Astiak. Soon, you will understand everything," Adina reassured him.

Astiak said, "Look, I come from a religious family, and none of these things you say make any sense."

Adina said, "Walk with me, dear Astiak."

Adina and Astiak started walking in the Barduk forest.

Adina began narrating a brief history that would help Astiak understand his present circumstances. "In the beginning, there were two beings, Mawu and Ahrima, two sources of energy. There were just them and nothing else. One day, they decided to create the universe, including your planet, so the great explosion happened. They used their divine art to shape everything. They started with the stars, then they created the planets, but everything was plain and void.

"They named the universe Galmadorian. There was no life

anywhere. They paid dearly for this creation since they spent most of their strength shaping and creating the cosmos. Ahrima was content with what they made, but Mawu wanted more: an entertainment. He wanted to create other creatures. Intelligent, sentient beings that could live, reason, and make their own decisions.

"Ahrima, in the beginning, was against his wish. She knew any creature would be corrupted and destroy their masterpiece, but she saw the eagerness of Mawu, and her endless love for Mawu made her accept and create Elohims like Melektav on twenty-four different planets in the universe with their remaining power. They were in charge of giving life freedom, the capacity to learn, and the capacity for earning, but Ahrima was correct—creatures made by Elohims were simple to corrupt, and one by one, they destroyed both their own planet and those of the others. Six were destroyed and eighteen planets remained.

"Ahrima warned Mawu that the corruption of lesser beings would result in the extinction of planets and, ultimately, the universe. Still, Mawu was blinded by the love of the Elohims for their creations, like a father. Ahrima never had such affection for other beings, so she proposed to make a challenge to test each Elohim in three different eras and, in case of failure, vanish all beings from the planet. The planets could be saved and worthy beings would remain there."

Astiak whispered, "So if the planets survive, will they survive as well?"

Adina answered, "Precisely. Mawu's love didn't allow him to destroy the failed societies. Therefore, Ahrima took this on herself. But something odd happened. With each annihilation, Ahrima gained more power as she devoured the ashes of lesser beings, and the Elohims and Mawu became weaker. Ahrima's greed for power changed her. Her love for Mawu faded out; instead, she became obsessed with the power that she was regaining."

"If you gaze long into evil, evil also gazes into you," Astiak commented.

Adina agreed with him. "Indeed. When Mawu realised it, it was too late. Nine more planets were destroyed. Only nine were left, including Dalanar, what you know as Earth. When he finally saw his beloved Ahrima becoming malicious and avaricious, he made three Haruns in each planetary sphere to guide the warriors through their trials. However, this was the last trace of his almighty power, rendering him ineffective and only an observer. Nonetheless, his hopes for his offspring remained firm and unbroken. We are almost there, Astiak."

At this moment, Astiak and Adina appeared from the trees of the Barduk forest and saw the others by the place where two rivers connected.

Branabus turned towards Adina and said, "Always a pleasure to see you, Adina."

Adina replied, "It's a pleasure to hear something positive from you, Branabus. Hello Antor, it's good to see you again."

Tahona and Astiak looked confused.

Baldor said, "Um yeah, she's talking to the voice in my head; his name is Antor. I am Constantine/Baldor; she is Scarlet, but they call her Tahona, and you are…."

"It's Astiak!" Astiak interrupted him.

"Hello Astiak," Tahona greeted.

Baldor said, "So… what should we do now?"

Tahona, sarcastically, replied, "I guess we are the redeemers of Earth."

Branabus disagreed with her. "Most unlikely. Endeavourers, perhaps."

"You are a Harun, Branabus! Not a prophet. They have been chosen by Melektav to save all beings on this planet. Her power and wisdom are beyond our understanding!" Adina rebuked

Branabus.
Branabus continued undermining Tahona and Astiak. "Indeed, yet the warriors of the last two millennia failed in their quests." Adina said ironically, "Your scepticism is poisoning the air, and that's all they need to begin their journey. The failure of the past warriors is neither their fault nor their destiny."
"The bitterness of truth makes it hard to swallow, my dear Adina. I agree that these warriors are different people, but don't forget this: the apple doesn't fall far from the tree. Lesser beings of Dalanar proved that they repeat the same mistakes over and over again. That's why we are at the brink of destruction and knowledge, which I give to begin the journey with, and I hope they succeed and find the divine truth, Melektav." Branabus responded. Turning to the warriors, he encouraged them, "Though my hopes are shallow, I wish you survive and save Dalanar from annihilation."
Tahona lost her patience and said, "This is all insane. I died half an hour ago and as soon as I opened my eyes, I found myself here and you tell me I have to save the planet without telling me how. Why was I chosen for this? You gave me a new name. You all look weird, like you jumped out of the fiction books, no offence. I think I'm going crazy."
Branabus was sympathetic. "Bear with me, Tahona. You will find your answers one by one. When Melektav created your seed from the ash of Aurelian, she named you Tahona and blessed you with her divinity, like all other living beings. At the end of each era, three warriors among the superior lesser beings of each planet are chosen to find the path to the salvation of the living on their planet. The warriors of the past two millennials came and failed."

Adina continued, "You were chosen by Melektav before you were born up there. All three of you had shorter life cycles than your own kind and died at the exact moment, not by natural causes."

"So she chose our deathtime, right?" Baldor was mystified.

"No, your choices in life brought death upon you. You know that very well, Baldor, but Melektav was aware of your destiny," Adina answered him.

Baldor put his head down and became quiet.
Tahona started shivering and said, "My mother told me, "Don't go in the rain." I should have listened. Who's going to take care of my daughter?" She started weeping silently.
Astiak got close to Tahona and whispered, "You shouldn't be worried about her. I'm sure she's fine and there are people taking care of her."
Baldor looked at Adina and asked, "What about other people? Animals? What happens to them after death? What about Leo, my dog? Is he going to be all right?"
Adina responded, "After death, they will go to Delatoar, a planet created by Mawu. Animals and all other non-dominant species on different planets, along with the best of your kind, go there."
Baldor added, "But he is still alive."
"He will live his life till then," Branabus said.

Adina addressed them, saying, "You are here now, ready to take the leap of fate and start your journey. Come forward and see."

The three warriors approached the hilltop ahead of them. They could not believe what they were seeing. In front of them, in the distance, a blue light beam began to shine. The light was emanating from a huge orb, half of which was hidden behind a mountain far away. From that distance, the mountain looked like a huge diamond and was covered with trees.

The blue, sun-like sphere gave light to the realm. Now they could see the plains, hills, and rivers. What an indescribable sight! In front of them, somewhere closer in that lower realm, there was a huge white tree that was as far as the eye could see, and the rest of it was hidden above the clouds. The warriors were stunned by the majesty and greatness of that tree. After a while—that could be a few seconds—they turned their heads to the right and saw a tree as tall as the one before, but this one looked as if it was burning in an infernal flame."

Baldor asked in astonishment, "What is this land called?"

"That is Belanor, the realm of Elohims, where you continue your journey," Branabus answered.

"What about that mountain?" asked Tahona.

"That is Mount Talazar, the mountain where Melektav's castle is situated. That is your final destination" Answered Adina.

"We are on top of a hill with a waterfall in front of us. It leads nowhere. Exactly how do we get there?" Tahona wondered.

Branabus answered, "This is your first step, Tahona. Where your journey begins with a leap of fate."
"So…" Tahona wondered.
Baldor interrupted her, remarking, "We need to get inside the river and let the waterfall take us wherever it will."

Astiak stepped into the river and vanished inside the waterfall in the span of a single blink.

Baldor looked at Tahona and said, "It's time to go, Tahona."

"Good luck, Tahona. I'll see you soon," Branabus urged her.

Tahona was worried. "But what if…."

Before Tahona finished her sentence, Baldor grabbed her hand and jumped into the turbulent river with her. The river was tumultuous and deep. They were sucked in and carried away from the falls by it. All they could see was the water. In a few seconds, they arrived at a location with turbulence, and the river quickly calmed down.

SHAJAR'ANAK

Tahona felt a hand grab and drag her from under the water. It was Astiak. While she was coughing, she heard Baldor coughing somewhere close to her. For a second, she looked around and found herself inside a pond. She looked up and saw the glistening waterfall that led them there. She saw that the Barduk Forest and the hill that they were there a few minutes ago was not a hill, but, it was a piece of land that was suspended in the air.

The pond was full of small golden fish the size of sardines swimming in it. The only difference was that something similar to wings was attached to both sides of the fish's body. There were several lotuses on the surface of the pond. Around the pond was uneven land covered with green grass, lilies, and orchids. But what enchanted the eyes more than anything else was the stout tree that they saw from the top of a small hill approximately fifty metres away from them.

None of the warriors had seen a tree with such grandeur, greatness, and beauty in their lives. The width of the tree was about thirty metres and its length was infinite and as far as the eye could see. That tree was white and covered with thick branches. Thousands of Nour birds were sitting on its branches, but this time they were not singing anymore.

Astiak turned to Tahona and asked, "Are you alright?"

Tahona pushed him back, charged towards Baldor and yelled, "You son of a gun! How dare you drag me along in that river with you? I could have died!"

Baldor smiled and said, "Die? Do you mean, again?"

Tahona looked confused and said, "We don't know that. I had a lot of questions and you two just took a leap in the dark without thinking. We don't know where we are going. We have no idea what we are going to face. Do you know this goddess? What does she look like?"

"I just did it because I felt I should do it. I didn't think about it," Astiak replied.

Tahona continued arguing with him. "Exactly. You didn't think. Now we are in the middle of nowhere and we don't know in which direction we should walk. Even those two weirdos are gone."

Astiak reminded her of their name, "Haruns."

"And they were three; Antor is here with me," Baldor said. Suddenly, a little further on the grass, particles started to shine in the air. Every moment, more particles shone and after a few moments, they formed two light spheres, approximately two metres long. At this moment, Branabus and Adina came out of the two spheres.
Tahona was shocked as Astiak and Baldor stared at them. Even though they were in a whole new world for a while, they continued to be amazed by things like that.

"Worry not, warriors; you will occasionally have our company," Branabus assured.

Tahona was shocked. "You terrified me! Also, why didn't you bring us with you if you could come here like this?"

Adina remarked, "It was not just an ordinary waterfall, Tahona. It was a river and you bathed in it so that you would be cleansed and purified for Shajar'anak."
"Who's that?!" Baldor shouted.
Suddenly, they heard a frightening roar akin to that of a lion.

The pond started quivering. It lasted only a few seconds until it became quiet, but it seemed longer.

Shajar'anak said, "O' Aeluminars."

They started looking at the tree where the voice was coming from.

Shajar'anak, with her dreadful yet calm voice, continued, "I am Shajar'anak, mother of all Shajars in Dalanar and Belanor."

"Antor said Shajars are trees," Baldor whispered.

Shajar'anak continued, "And three sage Haruns are here, too."

Branabus and Adina bowed their heads in genuine regard, expressing their deepest and most heartfelt respect for Shajar'anak.

"Greetings to you, mother of Shajars," Adina said first.

"Greetings, Lady Shajar'anak," Branabus followed.

Shajar'anak replied, "So, the time has come. This might be the beginning of the end, but no one, not even Mawu, can foresee the end of this. Uh, it was like yesterday when I saw the previous warriors. I never said this, but I liked Arda. I could see a fierce power inside him but he truly had a kind heart. Pity that they failed and caused their kin to become extinct."

Tahona bowed and said, "May I ask who those were who failed?"

"They were kins of Anthrolatus, a race similar to yours but taller, stronger, winged-like harpies and definitely not as beautiful as you, my dear Tahona," said Shajar'Anak.

Tahona's cheeks became red from Shajar'anak's compliment.

Astiak, with a polite tone, asked, "May I ask why they failed? As you said, they were stronger and could fly. If they couldn't succeed, then there's no chance for us."

Shajar'anak responded, "What defeated them was them, Astiak. Greed, wrath and grudges made them turn against each other. However, you should not be frightened by that. Their story is history now. You shall begin your journey but not without your gifts."

At this moment, three Nours flew towards Tahona, Astiak and Baldor from one of the millions of Shajar'anak's branches. Each one was holding something with their beaks. They left the gifts in front of each warrior and flew back to where they came from.

Shajar'anak said, "For you, Astiak, you will have the staff of Radice. May your roots remain as tenacious and deep as ever. Baldor, you are the Flame Bearer, so you will have Pasargad's flame sword. You shall incinerate the past and keep it where it belongs. And for you, Tahona, you will have the Moonlight dagger and the Umbra orb. I shall warn you about the power of the Umbra orb, as it may show the truth or lie. You'll be the one deciding to follow or dismiss the visions."
Tahona looked at the orb. It was bright purple. Inside the sphere, clouds like dust were constantly moving.

"Where should we go from here, Shajar'anak?" Astiak asked. Shajar'anak informed them, "You shall leave now and must find Namalmur Dune. Seek for Aland, the queen of Namalmur, but beware."
Tahona suspiciously asked, "Beware of what?"

Adina responded, "You never know how she will treat you."

Astiak thanked Shajar'anak, "Thank you… for the staff."

Shajar'anak replied, "You are welcome, young warrior. I wish you luck in finding the right path and hope you overcome the obstacles ahead of you."

They all said farewell to her and started walking. During all this time, Baldor was quiet. Astiak asked him, "Is everything all right?"
"Yes, maybe. I don't know. She chose to give me this sword. Flame-bearer. I mean, it's not on fire or something, but I don't understand why she called me Flame Bearer. I just don't like to think about it." Baldor answered.

Tahona heard their conversation and said, "Are you pyrophobic?"

"What? What the heck is that?" Baldor asked.

Astiak answered, "It's a Greek word, an extreme fear of fire. Baldor: I'm not afraid of fire. I just don't have good memories of it.

Tahona curiously asked, "And what are those memories?"

"Personal stuff, none of your concern!" Baldor replied coldly. His response dissatisfied Tahona. "We are dead and going on a journey together for God knows how long. We know nothing about each other. At least we can talk. I'll begin with myself. Hi, I am Scarlet, but here they call me Tahona. I was born in England but moved to Italy because of my job. I was a web designer and my life was good—well, I mean, apart from the fact that Daniele cheated on me. After that, I gave birth to our daughter, and I moved back to Leeds. After two months, I died while I was going back home."

Astiak, with a pitiful tone, said, "Sorry to hear that. What is her name?"

"Julia. She is with my mother now," Tahona answered.

Astiak assured her, "I'm sure she'll take care of her."

Astiak continued, "Ok, I'll go now. I'm Jacob; I mean, I was Jacob now, I'm Astiak. I'm from South Africa. I left my town and

continued my studies in the capital. After graduation, I was looking for a job but couldn't find anything in Cape Town, so I moved back to Pretoria. After many years of being away, I thought things had changed there, but the bullies who made my childhood a living hell didn't forget me. So once, when I was returning home from the grocery store, they saw me and started talking about the horrible pranks they had played on me. I tried to pass, but they stopped me. Just one moment, the only moment that I lost my temper in my life, when I stood up for myself, I tried to scare them with a bottle from the grocery store that I bought."
Astiak smirked and continued, "Well, that didn't go well. They beat the heck out of me. I closed my eyes there and opened them here.

Tahona solemnly replied, "Oh, that's sad."
"It is what it is," Astiak said.

Tahona asked further, "But did you ever stand up for yourself during your childhood? I mean, to fight back or something?"

Astiak said, "No, I was a quiet boy; I didn't have siblings or a father to protect me. As you see, I am not a tough guy, so I always tried to stay out of trouble. I let them finish their pranks. It was easier and faster."

"What happened to your father?" Tahona inquired.

Astiak told her, "He left us when I was four to find a job in Libya. He never came back."

"Did he die there?" Tahona wondered aloud.

Astiak replied, "When I grew up, I tried to find him via Facebook, and I did. When I texted him, he just blocked me. I saw that he had another son from another woman.
Tahona was angry. "Oh my god! What a jerk!"
Baldor advised Tahona, "Don't judge someone that you don't

know just because you heard a few words about his life."

"He left them and got married to someone else. It's crystal clear." Tahona said in defence.

Astiak said, "She is right. He was a jerk and I'll never forgive him for that. He wasn't there even when I died.

Tahona, facing Baldor, said, "We told you about us, now tell us about you."

"Did I ask you to tell me?" Baldor mocked.

Tahona was disappointed in him. "I just try to be friendly." Baldor, disinterested in this conversation, said, "And what if I don't want to?"

Tahona started crying.

This alarmed Astiak, who tried to calm Baldor. "Relax, man; there's no need to be bitter."

Baldor muttered, "Bitter!"

Haruns were a few steps behind them and were observing them. They were communicating through telepathy, so the warriors could not hear them.

Branabus, with a sad tone, said, "They can't get along from the start, and my expectations are poor. These warriors are nowhere near as excellent as the previous ones, yet they failed. I am concerned that all our efforts will be in vain."
Adina said sarcastically, "When was the last time you greeted the warriors with optimism? I believe in them because Melektav believes in them."

Branabus continued, "Look at them, Adina. Do you see any room for optimism? They haven't faced any challenges and yet they are at war among themselves."

Branabus sighed and continued, "They don't even know about Baldor's past. Do you think they'll stick together after learning about his past?"

Antor, for the first time with a whisper-like but firm voice, said, "Their fate is not in our hands, and it is not our concern either. Do not let your experience cloud your mind and assume their final destiny, Branabus. Haruns are aware of the past and present but not the future. We only need to provide them with a hint, then let them navigate through their own challenges and make their own decisions. Adina was pleased with Antor's short speech and had a smile on her face. Baldor was walking ahead of the others and then stopped at the point where the forest ended.

Tahona wandered across the forest, dejected and upset by Baldor's attitude. Astiak, still perplexed by Baldor's behaviour, attempted to break Tahona's train of thought by initiating random conversations until Baldor abruptly said, "Over there!"

ALAND

The end of the forest was followed by a flat area surrounded by two big mountains. It was around dusk. They all stared at where Baldor was pointing. In the distance, they noticed a dune. That hill had a peculiar air about it. They could not tell what it was due to the distance, but it was covered in black dots. Adina said, "That is Namlamur dune, the den of Aland."

"Who is she?" Baldor asked.

Branabus answered, "She is the queen of Namalmur; up there, you call them ants. She was created by the first Elohim, Melekmazut, at the same time as Shajar'anak. Both of them are interdependent, though their relationship has had its ups and downs. One thing you should bear in mind, she will not let you pass through her hill unless she gets what she wants."

"And what does she want from us?" Tahona wondered.

Astiak asked, "Do you mean by force?"

"No, with kindness," said Baldor sarcastically.

Tahona gave Baldor a stern look but said nothing.

Adina replied, "Yes, she will use her force."

"But I mean, we are dead, right? We are just souls; how can she harm us?" Astiak continued.

Adina smiled and replied, "Not exactly."

"So, we don't have a soul?" Tahona asked, looking confused.

Baldor then asked a follow-up question, "And there is no heaven and hell?"

Branabus replied, "Questions; Dalanar's superior lesser beings evolved more than other surrounding planets because of questions, but many of them were preposterous. You asked yourself questions and then you answered them. Answers that even surprised Mawu and Ahrima. Creating divine beings from your imagination, developing their characteristics and worshipping them en masse. That is fascinating. However, you never understood where you came from or where you will go simply because no one brings any memories from the past and no one has ever returned from death.

Baldor said mockingly, "Enlighten us then."
"When Mawu and Ahrima created the first Elohim, they gifted her a chest filled with the ashes of Aurelians. Those ashes were not ordinary. Those were particles of their essence. Elohims started creating Khaims, living creatures on Dalanar, from the dust. In the beginning, there were only unicellulars. Over time, these unicellulars evolved due to different conditions over thousands of years. Because of this, the Elohims created them in the same evolved form," Adina replied.

Tahona interrupted Adina and said, "So, is the theory of evolution true?"

"Yes," Adina confirmed.

Tahona happily said, "I knew it."

"But the final form was predefined by the Elohims. After the death of each particle, all Khaims, apart from Anthrolatus, Anthromeinis, and the last one, Kayans, your race, are sent to Del'ator, Mawu's utopia. These three races were the dominant species on Dalanar, and they used and abused all other Khaims; therefore, Mawu decided to have a judgement day for each individual to accept them in Del'ator or let them be devoured by Ahrima. And about you, you three are the chosen warriors. You do not follow the same pattern as the rest of the lesser beings. After your death, your ashes were brought back here, and you were reborn inside a Shajar. You are resurrected in your body before you die. However, you have other abilities…" Adina continued.

Suddenly, a distant voice rose and Adina's words were interrupted. They were so focused on Adina's story that they didn't notice they were approaching the dune. With the sound of a trumpet, they abruptly returned to reality and noticed the dune a few hundred metres away. Baldor had the flame sword firmly grasped in his right hand. Suddenly, something black started coming out of those holes in the dune. When they got closer, the warriors realised those black things were gigantic ants. The ants' faces were frightening at this size. An army of ants whose stature was the size of a big dog. They were armoured in emerald steel. The form of an ant wearing a crown was carved into their helmets. In one of their arms, they were all holding a bardiche. They came forward with exemplary order and stopped within a few steps of the warriors.

One of those armed ants, who was significantly bigger than the others and was wearing black armour, came ahead and said, "I am Dalaho, the commander of the Namalmur army. I welcome you on behalf of the queen. She is waiting for you in the emerald hall. However, I should inform you that according to the new rules in Namalamur, it is forbidden for Haruns to enter the Namalamur dune.
"But why?" Baldor asked.

Branabus informed him, "Haruns are not welcomed by Aland, queen of Namalmur, after our last encounter. She believes our presence will affect the minds and decisions of warriors."
"You can't let us go there alone while you know she may do something to us." Tahona whispered.

Branabus replied, "Rules are rules."

Branabus then whispered so only warriors could hear, "You should enter the dune and acquire the key to the Raionar's palace. It's a scroll. Don't forget that you must get it by any means."

Dalaho, in a stern and demanding tone, said, "Queen Aland does not appreciate unpunctuality. We must move now."

Fear and uncertainty were in the warriors' eyes. Just before they went, Adina said, "Use your gifts wisely."
The warriors started walking along the path that the army of Namalmur had opened for them. Their army consisted of tens of thousands of soldiers. All the soldiers were standing in their positions, straight, silent, and without the slightest movement. Astiak was observing the area and trying to predict what was waiting for them. Tahona was reluctant and concerned. She was trying to figure out why Aland hadn't let the Haruns in.

Just a metre away from her, Baldor was analysing their army. He was looking around to see if he could find a way to escape if things went south or maybe a weapon he could fight with, but the dune looked solid and the army of Namalmur seemed to be impenetrable. After a few minutes, they found themselves in front of the dune. There were many small holes on the hill, but in front of them was a big hole approximately two metres long. Dalaho shouted to the soldiers to halt, turned to the warriors and commanded, "Follow me!"

He entered the big hole and the warriors started following him. When they entered, they realised it was more like a tunnel made of soil. They continued walking until they could not see the light from outside. The inside of the cave was slightly lit by the torches hanging on the wall. But those torches were not lit by fire. The colour of that flame was green, and it was not moving. Suddenly, Dalaho stopped and shouted, "Anikse!"
Suddenly, green flames flared up on the wall and they saw in front

of them an emerald green gate that was emitting light. Maze-shaped patterns were carved on the gate. From the top of the gate and where the maze started, through a hole, a small creature in the shape of a beetle started to walk inside the maze and after a few seconds, it reached its end at the bottom of the gate, entered the small hole and disappeared. The gate started to open with a loud noise and a great hall was revealed to the warriors.

Dalaho started stepping inside the chamber and the warriors followed him. The warriors were able to see the chamber now. It looked massive enough to reach one hundred square metres and was semi-circular in shape. The room's floor, walls and ceiling were made of silver metal. The art and effort used to build that throne room in the heart of that dune were commendable.

The walls were ornamented with star-shaped windows that let in soft, ethereal light. On the walls in front of them, there were windows shaped like a crescent moon that guided the outside light into the room, but the main source of light was emitted from a huge emerald hanging from the chandelier, which decorated the whole room with green. A grand royal throne was placed at the end of the chamber. A giant ant was sitting on the throne.

Her gaze was fixed forward, steadfast and unyielding, implying a deep and unshakeable inner power. The warriors thought that must be Aland, the queen of Namalmur. Her shoulders were draped in an emerald-coloured cloak and she held a green staff in her left hand.

Twenty army ants were positioned on either side of the throne. These soldiers were significantly bigger than the ones they saw outside of the dunes. They had metal spears, and their armour looked more solid. Dalaho, who was leading the way, arrived at the throne. He bowed and said, "O' Aland, queen of Namalmur, I brought the warriors to your presence as you ordered. Aland, in a hushed tone, asked, "And what about Haruns?"

Dalaho responded, "They are left behind as you ordered."

"Excellent news, Dalaho! Those vagabonds have brought nothing but devastation to our chamber. Oh, I almost forgot about our guests," Aland gushed joyfully. She started observing the warriors individually and said, "You guys are the weakest Aeluminars I've seen. Dang, how does mother expect you to overcome the obstacles you'll be facing? You guys are lost. I bet you won't even make it halfway. You developed Dalanar to an outstanding level, but here, no way. Am I wrong, Dalaho?"

Dalaho bowed and responded, "Physically, they definitely are not comparable to Anthrolatus or even Anthromeinis, but I'm not sure about their capabilities, my queen."

Aland walked into the chamber and went to Tahona. She then held Tahona's arm with her tarsi and said to Dalaho, "Look at this one, she's so petite and fragile."

She then walked towards Astiak and asked him, "What about you? Do you think you can reach my mother? No, I don't think so!" She then went further and stopped in front of Baldor, checked him with her investigative black eyes and said, "Hmm, this one looks stronger. He must be Mano, but he is still not good enough."

Queen Aland then walked towards her throne and sat again. She said, "I am aware of your intentions; you need the permission scroll to enter Raionar's palace."
Her eyes were locked on Tahona. She then continued, "But you know well that everything comes for a price. I have something you want and you possess something I desire. It's going to be a fair trade."

Tahona and Astiak looked at each other, flabbergasted. They were wondering what she wanted from them. Aland continued: "Umbra orb, that's what I want."

The warriors looked at each other with doubt. Tahona was hesitant; she didn't want to give the orb even though she was not aware of its power, but at the same time, she thought that it might be very precious to Aland and that's why she was willing to give the Permission Scroll so easily in exchange for that orb.

Tahona was in her thoughts when Baldor, with an intimidating voice, said, "We will not give you the orb. We are here for that key and one way or another, we will get it."

Baldor's words astounded Astiak and Tahona.

"How dare you talk to me like that, Baldor?" Aland said in an aggressive tone.

Aland then ordered her soldiers, "Children, arrest these feeble Aeluminars and put them in the dungeons!"
Baldor took out his flame sword from its sheath and, with a swift swing, cut the ant soldier that was getting close to him in half. The battle began.

Tahona was still in a state of shock over everything that was happening, but Astiak was already beating the soldiers with his staff. Baldor fought like a natural warrior. He was moving like a feather in the chamber and defeating the soldiers one by one, but they were countless. Dalaho stepped forward and started fighting Baldor. The swords of the two warriors hit each other with strength and agility. They attacked each other with swords with all elegance, repelling the blows and dodging the other's attacks. None of them could get the upper hand.

Astiak spun his staff in the air and knocked the ants to the ground with exemplary power, as if he were a master of martial arts.

Aland, in anger, screamed, "Don't show mercy to these ruthless Aeluminars. Kill them all."

Tahona, in the meantime, had come back to her senses and dashed into action. She was moving like a fish between enemies and stabbing them one by one with indescribable skill and elegance.

But for every single enemy they defeated, two more foes replaced them to take their place and they were as ruthless and determined as the last. The warriors became tired, their arms heavy, and their spirits weak. They were engaged in a seemingly never-ending war.

Aland was sitting and observing the fight from her throne. After almost a quarter-hour of fighting, Astiak raised his staff in the air and shouted: "NOLITE OMNES". A mighty wind emanated from the staff. Roots started growing under their enemies' feet and pinned all the soldiers and Aland to the ground. Everyone in the chamber, including Baldor and Tahona, was surprised by Astiak's spell.

Ant soldiers were trying to escape, but with each move, the roots grew more on their bodies.
The warriors turned their heads towards Aland and started walking towards her. When they reached a few steps away from Aland, they heard her say, "That incantation was beyond your knowledge and power."
"You are right. Antor was with us all this time," Baldor said.

Aland whispered, "And I told them to keep everyone else away from my dune."
"We didn't want anyone to get hurt; your soldiers attacked us first," Astiak said.
Aland replied with loathing, "They are my children, all of them and you slaughtered them."

Baldor replied, "They were the ones that tried to kill us."

"If I wanted them to do so, I would've killed you before entering my chamber without you even knowing it," said Aland.

Tahona was shocked and felt sorry for what happened, "We didn't want this to happen."

"Don't waste your breath!" Aland responded with a look of hatred on her face. She then put her tarsi inside her robe, brought out the Permission Scroll and threw it in front of Tahona. She then continued, "Take this and get out of my chamber. Leave Namalmur and never come back!"

Baldor bent over and picked up the scroll from the ground. The scroll was rolled and the length was about thirty centimetres; it was made of papyrus and the knobs were like the face of a roaring lion.
Seconds after Baldor picked up the scroll, sparkling lights started glowing in the middle of the chamber. The lights began to spread and shape a rectangular door. When the door was completed, they were able to see Branabus and Adina. Baldor stepped forward and, before entering the gate, turned to Tahona and Astiak and said, "Enter the Portone."

Even though Astiak didn't know the meaning of Portone, he understood that Baldor was referring to the portal, so he followed him.
Tahona was ashamed of what happened and felt deeply sorry for Aland. She turned to her and said, "I am sorry." She then entered the Portone and vanished.

ARMY OF SCRAWNY MEN

After that, Tahona passed the doorway and found herself with the others. The Portone vanished behind her. She then turned to Baldor, sprinted towards him and knocked him down with a single punch in his chest.
"They didn't want to kill us. You made us massacre them, you filthy, heartless beast." Said Tahona to Baldor and after that, she turned to Haruns and said, "and you. You made us go there, told us to bring a damn scroll without telling us why you need it and made us murder those poor ants without any reason. They did not want to kill us."

"Perhaps you're right, Tahona; they wouldn't have killed you and your fellows, but you could've stayed captive for eternity in Namalmur dungeons." Said Branabus to Tahona. Then he looked at Baldor and said, "Baldor's reaction was spontaneous and reluctant, but his intentions were benign. You still don't know the value of the orb you're carrying, Tahona. That gift was given to you for a purpose.

The Umbra orb was made by Abrauth, Yalouth and Monator, three sorcerers of Ishta'ar in Siphorios temple. It was supposed to be a gift to Elohims to foresee the future, but in the last moment of its creation, Shak'zadurath appeared there and added his wicked essence of deception to the orb. At last, the orb was not showing the true vision of the future, and once in a while, it showed a false vision of something that Ahrima wished to happen. Still, no one could know which vision, so the Umbra orb turned into an imperfect artefact. Therefore, the sorcerers could not gift it to Elohims. However, it was still a powerful weapon because many would wish to have it despite its defects, including Aland, the queen of Namalmur."

Adina said, "Three sorcerers of Ishta'ar decided to give it to someone who was innocent and would not wish to use it under any circumstance. So, they gave the orb to Shajar'anak, queen of trees, mother of greens."

"She must have seen something in you that made her gift it to you, Tahona. The power of the orb can be lethal firstly because it can reveal the future. Secondly, because of its unpredictable nature and if it falls in the wrong hand, it can destroy everything," Said Antor.

"And who's this Shak'zadurath?" Baldor asked.

"Shak'zadurath or Zaloth are the names of the lord of deceit. He was created by Ahrima and sent to Earth to create chaos and destroy the equilibrium. His images in your realm spread hypocrisy, falsehood, and loath among your kind. His actual presence brought discord and mayhem upon us in Belanor. Brothers betrayed the sisters, kin forsook their blood, and incertitude lingered everywhere. Only a few remained loyal to their nature and kept their oath to Elohims." Adina responded.

At this moment, Branabus started to walk away from where they were, which was behind the Namalmur dune and go towards a way leading to a cliff. The road ahead was like an off-road and devoid of any trees. The cliff seemed to be a hundred meters away from them. It was around dawn. Everybody started following Branabus.

Adina continued, "At the beginning, Zaloth was the puppet of Ahrima and obeyed her commands, but after a while, he became so powerful that Ahrima released him from under her command

and allowed Zaloth to reign as he pleased. Ahrima was aware of Zaloth's nature and thirst for destruction. That's why she gave Zaloth independence to unleash his ultimate wrath.

"Up there, we call him Satan," Astiak remarked.

"What you know as Satan, Lucifer, Sheytan and many other names was, in fact, the misbegotten son of Zaloth and Nymeria," Andor replied.

"Was?" Baldor asked surprisingly.

"Who's Nymeria?" Astiak asked afterwards.

At this moment, they arrived at the cliff Branabus was walking towards. He then turned to the Warriors and said, "Questions are infinite, and time is short. You'll get your answers soon, but first, we need to pass through Barahut land to reach Raionar's palace. Nymeria was his wife before Zaloth abducted her."

As they stood on the edge of the cliff, a spectacular sight appeared before them. A vast plain where a raging river flowed from the top of the mountain on their left side. They slowly realised what was strange about it when they stared at that scene a little more. There were dozens of huts on the plains on both sides of the river. However, the huts on that side of the river, which were closer to them, were as if they had been burned by fire and the smoke rose from them to the sky. The trees were dry, broken and without branches or leaves. On the contrary, on the other side of the river, there were beautiful and stable huts and green trees and agricultural lands full of crops. It was a strange paradox to live on the opposite side of the river. Both sides of the river were connected by a brown wooden bridge.

Branabus said, "You need to go down the ladder; we will meet you down at the plain."
"Can't you transfer us with that portal you opened before?" Baldor

immediately asked.

"Portones are dangerous ways of transport for you because they can be traced by Zaloth if used frequently." Branabus responded.

"What if he traces us? Will he come for us?" Astiak asked.

Andor replied, "You are not a worthy opponent for the lord of deceit. He will send Nargorg, the shadow assassin, his servant, to hunt you down."

Baldor responded with a bold tone, "Let him come, I will cut him in half with my sword."

Tahona, with a sarcastic tone, said, "I bet you do."

Adina smirked and responded, "Your courage is admirable, Baldor. However, you can't defeat Nargorg easily. He was one of the seven assassins of Elmwood. They were the best of their kind. They were able to travel between this realm and yours in dire circumstances to help your kind. They were loyal to Elohims and Mawu, but due to a feud between them, Nargorg went rogue. He offered his service and loyalty to Zaloth and, in return, asked for the power to defeat his own kind."

Zaloth forged the Shadow Talisman for Nargorg. The Shadow Talisman was the doom of the assassins of Elmwood. They fought to the last breath against Nargorg, but the talisman made him invincible. That power came at a high price. He was now the puppet of Zaloth. He became his slave and had to obey what Zaloth desired.

At this moment, Branabus said, "There is no time to waste. We will see you down there."

Baldor had an unpleasant feeling about Branabus. His haste was not understandable. There were a million questions in his mind, but Branabus did not have time to answer any of them. How could they save the planet without knowing everything about it?

Astiak, on the other hand, was feeling that Branabus was right, and they should continue their path as fast as possible.

The Warriors started going down from the old wooden ladder. Baldor, as always, went first and then Astiak and Tahona followed him. They descended the ladder carefully because it didn't look strong enough to handle three people; they reached the bottom safe and sound.

"All along the way, Tahona was thinking about all that happened. She was still feeling guilty about what they did to Aland and her children. At the same time, she was thinking about the burden of the Umbra orb. She was wondering when and how she should use it. At the same time, she was having negative thoughts about Baldor. He was violent and obnoxious. Also, he was hiding his past from them. He seemed to have a skeleton in the closet.

Tahona's train of thought was disrupted by a whimpering sound. She was so lost in her thoughts that she didn't understand they arrived at the ruined village. Just a few meters away from them, there was a creepy thin man dressed in torn cloth lying on the ground and weeping like a cloud during spring. She said without hesitation, "He needs help!"

"He does. However, the help must come from within, not from us." Branabus answered.

Tahona went closer to the man and sat on the ground and asked, "What happened? Is there something we can help with?"

The man covered his face with his hands and, without paying the slightest attention to her, continued mumbling, "They abandoned their kin and left us to suffer. Ye shall see the scourge upon yourselves.

Tahona stood up and stepped back. She did not understand precisely what he meant but didn't feel good about it.

At this moment, they heard a crowd approaching from behind the ruined huts. After a few seconds, the Warriors saw a group of skinny people similar to the weeping one on the ground with torches and swords in their hands coming toward them.

Baldor immediately unsheathed his sword and was ready to fight. Adina stepped forward and told him, "You don't need that they are not coming for you."

As the group approached, their unintelligible whispers became closer and the Warriors were able to see them in detail. They had bony and withered faces. Their hair and beards were long but very sparse. Their lips were dry and cracked and they had eyes like the dead.

Their bodies were so thin that they were like victims of famine. Fragile and rusted swords were in their hands and some carried dim torches.

The only words that Warriors understood were "traitors". The weeping man stood up and joined that group.
They passed by the Warriors and continued their way toward the bridge.

Astiak started following them after they went on the bridge. Tahona and Baldor did the same after a few moments. The army of scrawny men crossed the bridge, marching towards the village on the other side of the river.

Astiak, Tahona and Baldor stopped walking in the middle of the bridge and stared at the scrawny men. At that very moment, a bird as big as a pigeon flew from above the Warriors and after doing a wheel in the sky, it slowly sat on the bridge's railing. After a few seconds, it started singing a sad melody.

The army started slaughtering the people of that village. Adina, with a sombre tone, said, "The people of Barahut land bear a resemblance to your kin. Anytime a war happens between them, they do the same here, giving the news of the upper realm. Siopilos, the first of your kind in Dalanar, got eternal life to witness the destiny of your people. Once upon a time, he was called by the name Adam till he came here to see the salvation or annihilation of your kind. In the beginning, he had hopes that his kind would be able to reach salvation, but each time, your kind failed. What you witnessed now was a war derived from greed, sloth, and denial, something that often happens in the upper realm.

"You are the reason for all of your difficulties and pain. The Elohims have given you abundant resources, yet you were unable to reconcile with your own offspring. Your refusal to share your belongings has sown the seeds of inequality, injustice, and unending bias among your fellow humans."
Astiak, who felt offended by all the blame on humans, said, "You said it yourself and Zaloth is the reason for our deception. He is the reason that we are like this. Who created Zaloth? Who appointed him to bring misery to humans?"

"Though no seed shall grow in infertile soil, your kind is prone to corruption," Branabus replied calmly.

"Zaloth just gave you a little push," said Adina.

Baldor replied with a smirk, "But aren't we the way Elohims created us? Maybe from day one, we were created faulty."

"You were created with freedom of choice. What you brought upon you is on you." Adina replied.

Meanwhile, Astiak, Baldor and Haruns were debating about the creation. Tahona was staring at the top of the mountain, where the river flowed from. She could see from a distance a not-very-tall man staring at them. Andor whispered in Tahona's ear, "That is Siopilos. He was observing another war between your kind until he noticed you."

Tahona asked, "Why is he called Siopilos?"

Andor responded, "Because he has been silent since he came here and is waiting and hoping for your kind to have peace among you. It's been millions of years, but he hasn't lost hope."

"You said he was the first of our kind. Is he the first Homo sapiens?" asked Tahona.

"No, he is the first of what you know as Homo habilis. The third blessed species blessed by Elohims." Andor replied.

"And who are these skinny people? Why did they attack the other ones?" asked Tahona

"Anytime a war happens in Dalanar, an illusionary image of their war appears here," Andor replied.

"So Siopilos has to see this and suffer?" Tahona inquired.

No, he just becomes aware of the war and the reason for it.

"So, this one was because of greed." Tahona asked.

Andor responded, "You got it right, Tahona."

"Who were the other two blessed species?" continued Tahona.

At this moment, a trumpet blew in the distance. The bird sitting on the bridge rail flew towards Lord Siopilos. Everyone stopped talking and turned to look in the direction the trumpet sound had come from. The sound came from somewhere along the bridge, from the top of the hill in front of them, with countless trees. They couldn't see what the source of that sound was.

Branabus broke the silence and said, "There lies Raionar's palace. Unfortunately, none of us Haruns can enter his garden as it is protected by elder magic that is beyond our power." He then started walking towards the forest where the sound came from, and the rest followed him.

"Raionar? Isn't he the one whose wife was abducted by Zaloth?" asked Tahona.

"You remembered well, Tahona. I need to warn you, especially you, Baldor, not to use any violence or power in front of him. No one has the ability to defeat him."

"Why are we going there? Don't lead us to a place again without telling us the purpose of it. We need to know what we should do." said Astiak.

Tahona was content with what Astiak said.

Branabus replied, "Indeed, we always let you know about everything we know. However, you are free to decide what to do and how to do it. Raionar, the hand of Elohim, is the king of wildlife and the son of the first Elohim."

"So he is the brother of Aland and Shajar'anak?" asked Tahona.

"Will he attack us for what we did to his sister, Aland?" Baldor wondered.

Branabus calmly responded, "Fear not, Baldor. He will not harm you for what you did. However, his persona is a blend of rage, might, and unpredictability."

They had arrived at a point where the woodland was in front

of them. The lush growth of trees and plants made the area impassable. They were still wondering where the trumpet sound came from. It was getting dark. The sun of Belanor was hiding behind Mount Talazar.

At that moment, Baldor went ahead and checked the forest, then said, "We can't pass through this; it is impossible."

"The gate to Raionar's palace is ahead of you. The forest is just an illusion. Only those who carry the Permission Scroll are allowed to enter and will be able to go through, so this time, you will be on your own. We will leave you behind and hopefully see you in the Shajar'atash forest. Raionar will guide you." Andor explained.

Baldor whispered, "From one forest to another, it seems we are in a reality show."

"It is time to go, Warriors. May the blessing of Mawu be upon you!" Adina said.

RAIONAR

Baldor was closer to the trees, he stepped forward with doubts and miraculously passed through the trees and bushes to another place. Adina was right; it was an illusionary wall. A palace designed like an ancient Roman palace could be seen about 300 metres in the distance. He turned around and saw a solid grey wall right where there were trees before. He couldn't see Astiak and Tahona. For a moment, he started panicking. He touched the wall to see if he could return, but it was just a rough, solid, impenetrable wall.

After just a few seconds, right where he was touching the wall to find his way back, the face of Tahona emerged. She passed through the illusionary wall and found her face touched by Baldor's hands. They locked their gazes on each other for a second or two. A lightning-like spark flashed through Baldor's eyes and heart. Tahona pushed his hand away and said, "What are you doing?"
Baldor was flustered by what just happened and responded, "N... nothing; I thought that the illusionary wall was blocked behind me and you were left on the other side."

"So, you missed her? I mean, us?" Astiak, a few metres away from them, asked with a smile.

Both Baldor and Tahona turned their faces towards Astiak. Baldor responded, "No, I was just worried."
"Uh, I got it," Astiak, with an even bigger smile, responded.

Tahona felt weird about what just happened, and Baldor was on the same page too.

Astiak started looking around. The first thing that caught his attention as he looked around was the palace at the end of the garden. Its cream-coloured stone facade gave the palace a sense of elegance, stability, and beauty. A beautiful cream-coloured stone fountain was in the middle of the courtyard leading to the palace. In the middle of the fountain was a beautiful woman's figure, and the water flowed from her right hand, pointing towards the sky, and poured into the pond. The figure's eyes were closed, and in her left hand, there was something like a book, which he stuck on her chest. The roads leading to the palace passed on both sides of the fountain. The two roads were made of cream-coloured tiles and were covered with well-trimmed and beautiful bushes and flowers on both sides. The warriors walked towards the palace and after a few minutes, they reached the stairs leading to the palace. They wanted to go up the stairs, but a childish and funny voice caught their attention.

> "Trim the bushes,
>
> Cut the grass.
>
> When you finish
>
> Water them at last.
>
> Add more manure
> You will harvest more."

They went to where the sound was coming from: behind a wheelbarrow. They slowly approached the sound and saw a strange creature trimming a bush. The creature with its back to them looked like a child wearing a beaver hat.

"What is that?" Baldor asked.
The creature let out a short scream and turned its head towards the warriors. That creature was something like a giant mouse. He had big, cute brown eyes and was about seventy centimetres tall.

He was wearing a cotton suit. Because of his sudden move, his hat fell to the ground right in front of Tahona.

While grabbing his heart and panting, he said, "What's wrong with you? I could have had a heart attack."

Tahona immediately picked up his hat from the ground and went towards him, saying, "We are really sorry. We didn't want to scare you."

"You don't need to apologise, young lady. One of these two tough guys wanted to kill me," the mouse responded.

"We apologise. We don't want to kill anyone." Astiak responded. "We clearly stepped on the wrong foot. I was just surprised. I'm Baldor, by the way; this is Astiak and she's Tahona."

Tahona helped the mouse stand up. He started dusting his hat, put it back on his head and said, "I know who you are, dummy. Do you think we are having human guests in the house every day?"

Baldor and Astiak tried to control their laughs. Tahona asked, "May I ask your name?"

"Thank you for asking. My name is Booch."

"Nice to meet you, Booch." Tahona replied.

Booch, this time, responded softly, "Pleasure is mine, Tahona. Your manners are noticeable, just like your beauty," he then looked at Astiak and Baldor and continued, "These two should learn from you."

Even though Booch's tone was harsh and unkind, it did not bother Astiak and Baldor at all. In their eyes, Booch was like a grumpy little kid.

"What do you do here?" Tahona asked.

"I'm the gardener of Raionar. I was busy with gardening until you guys came. Everyone knew you'd come; they just didn't know when." Booch replied.

Astiak was surprised. "Everyone?" she asked.

"Krendale, guardian Gargoyles, sisters of nature, Raionar and I," Booch responded.

"Who's this Raionar? We should meet him," wondered Astiak.

Booch responded, "Raionar is the trueborn son of the first Elohim, Melekmazut."

"And what should we do with him?" Astiak asked.

"You ask a lot of questions, Astiak. You have to meet him yourself to understand."

"Is he cool?" Baldor asked.
"Cool as a cucumber," Booch answered.

Baldor smiled, looked at Astiak and Tahona, and said, "I like this guy. He's fun."
"Don't get fresh with me. I don't know if I like you or not," said Booch.
"Baldor continued, "That's exactly why I like him."
Tahona said, "Thanks, Booch, for your help. Can you please tell us where we can find Raionar?"
Booch bowed shortly and said, "Anything for you, fine lady. To meet Raionar, you need to go up those stairs and enter the gate in front of you. You'll meet him inside the palace.
"At first, he might look a bit intimidating, but you'll be safe with him." Booch then whispered.

Astiak extended his hand to shake hands with Booch and said, "Thank you, Booch. Wish us luck."

Booch cleaned his hand with his coat, shook Astiak's hand and said, "You're welcome, Astiak. I hope you can reach your destination and save this planet. Good or bad, it is our home, and you should do your best to keep it safe."
"Will we see you again?" asked Tahona.
Booch looked at Tahona and said, "Fate may cross our paths again, young lady."

The Warriors said goodbye to Booch and started walking towards the stairs. They walked up the stairs and saw the gate in front of them when they reached the last stair. Only then did they notice two stone sculptures on each side of the gate. The sculptures were like two Renaissance soldiers. Their bodies were covered with armour and steel helmets. The one on the left was holding a long spear in his right hand and the one on the right was leaning on a long sword. The warriors continued their way towards the gate and entered the palace.

As soon as they entered the palace, the gate slammed shut with a horrifying sound. After a few seconds of confusion, they noticed in front of them a large silver-coloured corridor leading to stairs, with two little gold and black doors on the left and right sides of the hall. The floor of the massive palace was covered in black tiles, with a stunning portrait of a girl's face carved in the centre. Tahona, Astiak and Baldor began to stroll inside the hall. Tahona took a right. There were different paintings on the wall, the largest of which was a depiction of a beautiful girl at the top of the steps. A little, miserable image of a weird creature was next to the small door on the right. The creature's face was like a bony toad, with aged skin, untidy hair and a face full of grief and despair.

This portrait was completely in contrast to the beautiful girl's portrait. Although she had a bony face, her figure appeared robust in the portrait, and her eyes were just as black as her long, straight hair. She looked even more stunning with her charming black lipstick. Baldor was mesmerised by the image of the girl and without pausing to think, he began to walk towards the stairs so that he could have a better look at the portrait. However, a terrifying roar suddenly erupted just as he approached the first step. A thunder-like roar rumbled through the hallway.

They were seized with fear, and they dared not speak. They could not believe what they were seeing. Their tongues were tied with fear and their eyes were wide with surprise.

They had never heard a description of the greatness of the creature that was in front of them, even in stories.

Lord Raionar was an enormous creature. His height reached four metres. His head was a tiger's, and his muscular torso was like a giant human body. His legs were like the legs of a giant goat. From that angle, they could see his bat-like wings. Raionar looked majestic, tremendous, powerful, and terrifying. His eyes were red like an inferno. On his head was a golden crown, in the middle of which was a diamond the size of a palm. His sturdy arms were covered with black hair and on his waist was a leather belt in which a huge blue sword was sheathed. An ornamental cloth was covering his private parts up to his knees. Raionar let out another skin-searing roar when he saw the three Warriors.

Yes, Adina was right. The three warriors couldn't fight Raionar, even if they wanted to.

Raionar started walking down the stairs. The frightening sound of his hooves echoed in the hall. He walked down with poise and elegance. When he arrived at the bottom of the stairs, he stood still. An ear-splitting silence reigned in the hall.

"At last. The last warriors of Belanor. Why do you wish to reach

Melektav?" Raionar asked in his horrifying voice.

The three Warriors were taken aback by Raionar's straightforward question. They did not know precisely why they should do all this or why they should meet Melektav. They just knew that their failure would result in the extinction of humanity on Earth.

Baldor bowed gently and responded humbly, "We still have people up there that we care about."

Raionar turned his head, gazed into Baldor's eyes and said, "Hmm, people? Your daughter died in the hospital; she was the last one of your kin that you cared about."

Baldor seemed as if a dagger had been thrust into his heart. He replied, "Leo, my dog. He is neither a human nor my kin, but he is the only one I still care about. Tahona has her daughter and mother up there and I don't wish anyone to die."

"And do you really care about your kind? Those doctors who refused to operate on your daughter because of your insurance? They led you to rob that shop. Your friend was killed, and you bled to death. You died and your daughter died on the same day. Now tell me, do you really care about the people up there?" Raionar said.

Tears flowed from Baldor's eyes and ran down his beard. All the while, Astiak and Tahona watched in astonishment as Raionar told the truth about Baldor's past. It all sounded like a psychological game by Raionar.

Raionar continued, "Don't forget that up there, there are people way worse than those doctors or police officers that shot you. Murderers, dictators, and abusers are just a few examples of the ones that will survive. You will do them a favour. Do you still want to help them stay alive?"

Raionar turned his head to Astiak and said, "What about you? Those guys that beat you and sent you here will survive. Your father will stay alive with his second family and live a happy life with them without even understanding that it was you who saved him. Do you think humanity deserves to stay on Earth? Maybe it's better to let them become extinct. Maybe it's just the time. Maybe the most corrupt, self-centred and destructive kind should go."

Raionar then turned his back to the Warriors and started going back from the stairs. While walking, he stopped for a second and said, "You are the chosen ones by Melektav. You may stay in my palace as long as you want. May you choose the right path.

Raionar's majesty continued to astound the Warriors and his thoughtful questions baffled them. Among them, only Tahona had a reason and purpose to continue this vague journey: her family. She would do anything to save her daughter's and her mother's lives. She would do anything for her daughter. Astiak cared about mankind. Even though people he knew weren't kind to him, he did not want all humanity to disappear. He felt responsible. Baldor, on the other hand, was full of loathing and anger. The only reason he had for living was his daughter, who was gone.

For a few seconds, the Warriors were lost in their thoughts. They were thinking about Raionar's questions until they heard a door open. They turned their heads towards where the creaking was coming from. It was the door next to the toad portrait. After a few seconds, they saw the same frog from the portrait walking inside the hall. The face looked the same as the portrait, but his body was the size of a normal human body. The toad was wearing a green royal robe. In his right hand, there was a black cane that he was leaning on. His hair was longer and messier than in the portrait. He then stopped and stared at the three Warriors one by one with a scrutinising look; then he whispered with a whizzing sound, "Hmm, thus ye are the last warriors of Belanor. Ye seem weary

and hungry. Ye must need somewhat to eat."
Astiak leaned towards Tahona and whispered in her ear, "Why does he speak like my grandma?"

Tahona uncontrollably let out a loud laugh. Baldor turned his head and gave a surprised look to Tahona. He was at the same time content to see her laughing, as it was the first time she had done it.

The toad muttered and said with a disappointed sound, "It's a pity that your educational system failed you. I'll speak in a way that's more familiar to you. My name is Krendale, counsellor and old friend of Raionar, the hand of Elohim."

Tahona, who was trying to control her laugh, started clearing the tears from her eyes. Astiak, with an apologetic tone, said to Krendale, "My apologies, this is the first time she's laughing since I met her."
Krendale, with an assuring tone, said, "No need to apologise, Astiak. It is completely normal for her to express her emotions louder than you two. In the end, she's the Lev, the heart of Astiliath."

Baldor, with a confused tone, mumbled, "Another weird name."

"Every name here will be weird for you, Baldor, because every greater being in Belanor speaks in 'Altomanos'," Krendale responded calmly. "We can speak your tongue as well, but there are no equivalents for the names in the upper realm, Dalanar, and about Astiliath, it is the unique ash of Elohims that each one of them possessed only one. These ashes contain three particles: Lev, Mano, and Zehn. Zehns are the mind, the thinker part of Astiliath, a gift from Mawu. You are Zehn Astiak.
"Baldor, you are Mano, the power given by Ahrima. And you, Tahona, are the Lev, the heart of Astilliath, the core of emotions and the gift from the last Elohim, Melektav. All three parts of Astilliath were forged by the current Elohim, Melektav. In Belanor,

you are called Aeluminars, which in Altomanosian means 'Light Bringer'."

"But I still don't understand; why do we need to find Melektav?" Tahona asked.

Baldor immediately continued, "Yes, I mean, what do we get?"

Krendale, with a weird facial expression that might be considered a smile, said, "Baldor, expectations are one of the basic characteristics of humans. One of the main reasons for your progress and regression. The reason for Raionar's pessimism towards you is the institutionalised self-centredness in your race."

"Raionar was right. I lost my daughter up there. I am dead. Just give me one good reason why I should go through this journey. Why should I care about humanity when they did not care about my daughter?" Baldor responded with a rough tone.

"I did not ask to see what I would get for it, Baldor. I asked to see what the purpose of this journey is and how it's related to saving all those up there or maybe having the possibility to go back or even seeing your daughter, but if you are a crybaby who wants to whine about your past, suit yourself!" Tahona responded aggressively.
Tahona's words startled Baldor. He became quiet and went into deep thought. Even though he lost everyone that he loved, he really didn't wish for the annihilation of the entire planet.

"I'm afraid to inform you that there's no way to see your daughter or Baldor's," Krendale said

Tahona started staring at the floor.
Krendale continued, "The main reason you need to reach Melektav is to get ready for the final battle."

"Battle with whom?" asked Astiak.

"With Shak'zadurath, lord of deceit," Krendale answered

"But I thought we only needed to reach there. No one said anything about any battle." Baldor said.

"You are right, Baldor. Your initial task was to prove yourselves by overcoming the tasks and obstacles, reach Melektav and give her the Astiliath so she can survive and keep anything on Dalanar and Belanor alive." Krendale responded.

"And how will we give Astiliath ash to Melektav?" asked Astiak.

Krendale rubbed his chin and said, "That would've been your last task, to sacrifice yourselves for all the other beings. However, now everything has changed. You should go to Melektav and prepare yourselves to fight against Zaloth."

"And Mawu is aware of these plans of Zaloth and Ahrima?" asked Baldor.

Krendale replied, "He is dormant now to regain his power. When he will be awakened is not clear to anyone."

"Let's say we reach there, fight and defeat Zaloth. What will happen after?" Astiak asked.

"I cannot answer that question because I'm not aware of what she will decide," Krendale responded.

He then started walking towards the stairs and said, "You are hungry and tired. I'll guide you to your rooms. You can take a bath and get ready for supper, which will be ready soon."

Krendale then continued walking up the stairs and the Warriors followed him in silence. They were thinking about what would be ahead of them, drowning in their thoughts till they reached

the landing. Baldor, Astiak and Tahona stopped there for a few moments and looked at the charming portrait of Nymeria. Astiak and Tahona continued their ascent up the stairs, but when they looked up, they stopped.
Astiak whispered, "Baldor."

Baldor was engrossed in looking at the portrait and didn't hear him.

Astiak repeated louder, "Baldor."
Baldor turned around to see what he wanted and said, "What?"
He then looked up and saw, on the highest staircase, three tall girls standing.
The beauty of those three girls was indescribable.

The girl on the right side; her face was as white as snow, her eyes were green, and her long hair started from the back of her head and covered her shoulders, her chest and reached her knees. She wore a long, stunning green dress with scales like fish skin.

In the middle was a girl with black skin and curly hair. Her beauty was as if she were an angel from heaven. She was wearing a long sky-blue dress and stared at them with big blue eyes. Her white wings could be seen even from that angle.

On the left was a brunette girl with light brown, wavy hair. Her eyes were black like the night and her lips were red like pomegranate seeds. The height of all three girls was the same—less than two metres. There was something special about their faces.

"They are daughters of Nymeria and Raionar," Baldor whispered.

"I think I'm in love," Astiak whispered back.

Tahona smiled and asked, "With which one?"

"I don't know. I don't care." Astiak answered.

Baldor said, "You don't have a chance, bro."
"How come?" Tahona curiously asked.

Baldor, with a serious tone, responded, "They are daughters of Raionar. Do you remember him? We are lucky that we are still alive. If he finds out we had an eye on his girls, dude, he's gonna rip us apart."

The three Sisters of Nature turned their backs and walked away.

Krendale, who was two stairs ahead of them, said, "They are Maral, Armia and Nilou and you are right, Baldor, they're daughters of Nymeria and Raionar. Maral, the one in green, is the protector of the aquatic. Armia, the one with the black dress, is the protector of the birds and Nilou is the protector of the terrestrials. It is normal for you to fall for them, Astiak. You were always fond of nature and wildlife; let's not forget that their extraterrestrial beauty also plays a role.

They followed Krendale up the stairs and went to the right. There were many doors in the corridor. Krendale first showed them Tahona's room, then Baldor's room and finally Astiak's room and sent them to their rooms to take a shower and rest.

The rooms of the Warriors were very luxurious and magnificent. The walls and ceilings of the rooms were made of gold, and they had luxurious and large wooden beds with ornamental carvings in their bedrooms. Inside the bathroom, a huge gold tub was filled with hot water and the pleasant aroma of wood filled the space. Tahona and Astiak were very happy alone in their aristocratic rooms. After a long shower, Tahona went to bed in her room and fell into a deep sleep.
After a warm bath, Astiak went to his bed and found a book on it —the book of Elden Sorcerers, Anaktarios. He started reading the book and after an hour or two, he fell asleep.
Still thinking about Raionar's words, Baldor reluctantly took a

short shower, went to his bed and stared at the golden ceiling. He constantly thought about Raionar and Krendale's words until he fell into a deep sleep.

Tahona woke up the next day. She was so tired that she did not notice the passage of time. She found new clean clothes next to her bed, it was a green hoodie like robe. After putting on the hoodie and washing her face, Tahona came out of her room. Outside the room, Krendale was waiting for her.
"I hope you had a good sleep last night, Tahona." Krendale greeted.
"Yes, it was amazing. Thank you, Krendale. I really needed it after such an exhausting day." She replied.
"I'm glad to hear that," answered Krendale.

Tahona asked, "Where are the others? I should wake them up."
"There's no need for that. Astiak and Baldor are already in the guest room." Krendale answered.
"Why didn't they wake me up?" asked Tahona.
"Astiak woke up a few minutes ago and joined Baldor, who had been awake for the past hours. They didn't want to disturb you. Now let's go and join them." Krendale replied.
Krendale started walking and Tahona followed him. After passing through several corridors, they reached the banquet hall, which was very luxurious and aristocratic. There was a long wooden dining table in the middle of it, and a huge chandelier was hanging from the ceiling, giving light to the room. At the end of the dining table, Raionar was sitting on a huge chair that looked like a king's throne, with Baldor sitting next to him and Astiak next to Baldor. On the other side of the table, the Sisters of Nature were sitting and eating their meals without saying a word. She noticed that Baldor and Astiak were wearing new clothes as well. Astiak was in a long, blue wizard-like robe. Baldor's new outfit however looked more fascinating. He was dressed in green . His forearms and shoulders were covered by metal armour
After realising Tahona's presence, Raionar said with a solemn

voice, "Good morning, Tahona."

Tahona, in a shy tone, said softly, "Good morning."

Tahona walked into the banquet hall and sat on the chair next to Astiak. Everybody in the room was staring at her.

"We had an unpleasant introduction yesterday, which was derived from my scepticism. I had a long discussion with your fellow, Baldor. My concerns are long gone now."

Tahona, with contentment and enthusiasm, looked at Baldor and then Astiak.

Raionar, with a kind tone, continued, "Enjoy your morning meal, Tahona. You must continue your journey afterwards."

Tahona, without saying a word, nodded with a smile and started filling her plate with slices of bread, fruits and vegetables that she didn't even know their names and started to eat eagerly. After half an hour of eating, Tahona looked at Raionar and said, "Thank you very much for the breakfast."

"You are very welcome. Your satchels have been filled with supplies for your journey." Raionar replied.

"Where are we heading to?" Tahona asked.

Raionar responded, "You need to go to Shajar'atash. Haruns will meet you there and from there, they will lead you to my brother, Aramashasb. He will lead you to pass through nefarious marshes to reach Esfalonar."

During all these conversations, the Sisters of Nature were silent. Raionar stood up from his throne-like chair and led the way. Astiak, Baldor and Tahona started following him. They left the banquet hall and after passing many corridors, they reached the stairways before their bedrooms. Raionar went down the stairs and stopped at the landing, right in front of Nymeria's portrait. He closed his eyes and after a few seconds, the great portrait started opening from the middle. That portrait was actually a gate to a Portone. After the gate was fully opened, they saw absolute darkness in front of them. A darkness that no light could penetrate.

Raionar turned to the Aeluminars and said, "You shall enter this Portone made by my Nymeria. Here we say farewell, Aeluminars. Don't forget to convey my regards to my brother. May the blessing of Mawu be upon you!"

The warriors looked at each other in surprise and fear. Krendale appeared from the top of the stairs and walked down towards them. He handed the Aeluminars their sachets and said, "I filled your sachets; you'll have supplies till you reach Lord Aramashasb."

Astiak, Baldor and Tahona bowed to Lord Raionar. Astiak said, Thank you, Lord Raionar."
Baldor said, "Thank you and I hope to meet you again."

"We will, Baldor," Raionar responded.
Baldor turned to Krendale and said, "Thank you, Krendale, you've been very kind to us. We didn't see Booch again. Please tell him that we said goodbye."
"Yes, please; I wish we could have more time with him. He is a gentleman," Tahona said.
At this moment, Baldor stepped into the darkness and Tahona and Astiak followed him inside the portrait.

SHAJAR'ATASH

After stepping into the darkness, they began to fall into an infinite, dark space. The three warriors started shouting, but none could hear the others. After a few seconds of falling, they stepped on solid ground. They found themselves in a wasteland covered in flames. The only visible thing was the scorching tree, which they first noticed when they were on top of the hill in the Barduk forest. As far as the eye could reach, there was flat land. The Warriors did not know where they should head.

Baldor, trying to hide his fear of fire, took a deep breath and said,

"I think we should avoid that tree. I feel something evil in it."

Astiak, while staring at Shajar'atash, responded, "I agree. Something is not right about that tree."

"I agree, but Raionar said our path goes beneath Shajar'atash. Do we have an alternative option?" Tahona asked.

"No, you're right. Let's just get the hell out of here as soon as possible. I don't like fire." Baldor responded.

"What about Haruns?" asked Astiak.

Baldor responded, "It seems that they bailed on us. We must continue without them."

He said this and started to walk towards Shajar'atash. Astiak and Tahona, without saying a word, followed him. The flames were scattered on the ground. Baldor carefully tried to go to the part where fewer flames were on the ground. They were a hundred metres away from Shajar'atash.

OKH'HON ZI SHOMAALEMO AELUMINARHA

The last weak Aeluminars.

OHOD RO SHAK'ZADURATH AKHO GOLAAD

The Wrath of Shak'zadurath is upon you

For a second, silence prevailed. The Aeluminars looked at each other, consternated. They were trying to figure out what that meant. After just a few seconds, a deafening scream rose from the sky. The scream was coming from the south. They started looking for the source. They saw a giant black bird in the sky flying towards them. They knew that this was not good news for them.

Baldor drew his sword from its scabbard and shouted, "Get ready for the battle! That bird doesn't look friendly."

Astiak was holding his staff of wizardry with both hands and was ready to fight. Tahona hoped the bird was an ally, but she was prepared.

The closer the bird got to them, the bigger it got.

That bird was the size of a small aeroplane. Her head was like the head of a bearded vulture. Her crown was covered with silver feathers, but all the other parts of her body were covered with black feathers. Her eyes, red like dancing flames, looked piercing and scary. Her wings were like the wings of a bat and she had put them on the ground. But there was no feather on her leg. Those were like the legs of an eagle but covered with scales.

A few moments after landing on the ground, the bird neighed like a horse and brought down her head. At this moment, they were able to see the person who was riding the bird. A spectre-like man descended from the neck of the bird. He looked 2 ½ metres tall. His build was slender. His face was like that of a soulless old man, covered with a long white beard. His eyes were as white as his hair. He was clothed in a black cloak. At the end of his long cloak, a dark fume was emitting. His chest was covered with black metallic armour. There was a palm-sized white talisman hanging around his neck. In his right hand, he was holding a long sword. A blue-coloured rope was wrapped around the sword. It looked like a whip. When he landed on the ground, the man started walking towards them while muttering unintelligible words under his breath.

"Who is he?" Tahona asked.

"I think he is Nargorg," Astiak whispered.

"I don't know who he is, but I'm sure he is definitely up to no good!" Baldor shouted.

Baldor then charged towards the man. He was holding his flame sword with both hands, unlike Nargorg, who held his in one hand. Baldor landed a powerful attack with his sword, but Nargorg deflected it with a swift swing. Sparks of fire and ice emanated from their swords. In no time, Baldor swung his sword again, but Nargorg deflected this as well and immediately kicked Baldor in the chest with his metal sabaton. That kick was so powerful that Baldor was thrown tens of metres away and his sword landed next to him. This time, Tahona charged towards Nargorg with her dagger. At the same time, Astiak raised his staff and cast a spell that he learned from the book of Elden Sorcerers, Anaktarios, and shouted, "THAKHADOR!"

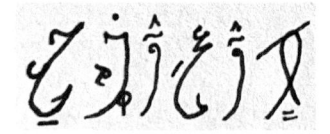

The spell hit Nargorg and froze him in place. Astiak was satisfied and happy with his work, but his contentment didn't last more than a second. Nargorg shattered the ice and freed himself. In the nick of time, he pointed his sword towards Tahona. The whip stretched out, grabbed Tahona by her wrist, swung her in the air and threw her on Astiak. Baldor stood up and grabbed his sword. He understood that he couldn't defeat Nargorg if he attacked him blindly, so he took a deep breath, disciplined his emotions and started walking towards Nargorg. He was holding his sword in front of his face. This time, Baldor didn't attack Nargorg; instead, he waited for him to attack. Nargorg wielded his blade artfully and Baldor swayed his attack and moved around him. Nargorg landed another attack from the right, but Baldor parried his attack. He then tried to feint him, but Nargorg predicted his trick and dodged his last attack. The whispers of Nargorg became louder at this moment and he charged towards Baldor with cleaving attacks, one after another. Baldor parried two attacks with the leftovers of his power, but he could not handle another one.

Astiak grabbed his staff and, with all his power, shouted, "SHLOKHAN!"

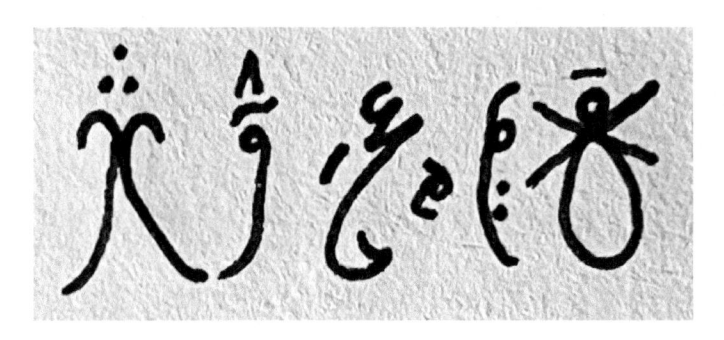

Nargorg had his sword in the air and was ready to land his deadly cleave on Baldor, but Astiak's spell hit him on the back. He howled in pain, turned his back to Baldor and faced Astiak. Tahona found the right moment to throw her dagger at Nargorg. Her dagger flew like a falcon towards Nargorg's heart, but the giant bird, who was only observant until then, swung her lioness-like tail and blocked the dagger. She then neighed, stood on her feet and started to charge towards Tahona, but Nargorg bellowed, "They… are… mine!"
The bird bowed shamefully and stepped back.

At that moment, a few metres away from Astiak and Tahona, a Portone was opened. After a few seconds, Booch stepped outside the Portone, smashed a small piece of glassware in his hand and immediately screamed, "AGNATH ZO LAM!"

At this moment, Booch's spell surrounded Nargorg in an orange

bulb and completely paralysed him.
Booch shouted, "We don't have time; enter the Portone now!"

After seeing his master captivated, the giant bird started pecking at the bulb with her beak. With each peck, the sphere started shattering little by little. Baldor picked up his sword from the ground and ran towards Astiak and Tahona. He grabbed Tahona's hand, and they all started running towards the Portone. Suddenly, Tahona let out a short scream and said, "My dagger; I forgot to bring it."
Baldor instantly released Tahona's hand and shouted, "Go now! I'll bring it." He then tossed his sword to Tahona and ran towards the dagger.
Tahona angrily shouted, "Come back! You'll get yourself killed."

Baldor didn't listen to her words. He ran towards where the bird deflected the dagger, which was right behind her. The bird was still pecking at the sphere, trying to release her master.

Baldor sneaked behind her and leaned to pick up the dagger from the ground. The bird noticed Baldor. She wagged her tail and hit Baldor in the chest. He was thrown tens of metres away from Portone, but he held Tahona's dagger like his life depended on it. The bird started bolting towards him and as she arrived where he was, she attacked him with her beak. Baldor crawled backward on the ground and dodged her attacks. He rolled left and when he found the right moment, he stabbed the bird in the right eye. The bird neighed earsplittingly and, while bleeding dark-coloured blood, walked backwards. Baldor knew it was the right moment to run back towards where the Portone was. Astiak and Tahona were standing by the Portone, shouting, "Come on, Baldor, run faster!"

Baldor reduced his speed because he thought he was safe, but right before reaching the Portone, something frozen grasped his leg. He looked to see the reason and realised it was the whip of Nargorg. He then turned back and saw Nargorg holding his talisman with his left hand. He was shattering the sphere and releasing himself. With his right hand, he held his sword, pointing at Baldor. He heard Tahona let out a scream. She took Baldor's sword in her hands and cut the whip from where it was grabbing him. Astiak then grabbed the back of Baldor's clothes and dragged him inside the Portone. After a second, Tahona entered as well, and they heard Booch snap his fingers and the gateway disappeared right away. Baldor, while panting, smiled at them and said, "That was close."

Tahona furiously screamed, "Are you out of your mind? You were about to kill yourself for a dagger."

Baldor opened his mouth to say something in his defence, but before he could say anything, Booch said, "That's not an ordinary dagger. That's…"

Before he finished his sentence, Astiak, Baldor, and Tahona jumped on Booch and hugged him tightly.

"We can't thank you enough, Booch," said Astiak.

"If it wasn't for you, we would've been dead dead by now," Baldor added.

Booch looked confusedly at Baldor.
Tahona tried to explain, "He means dead again. You got it? Because we died once…"

Booch said, "I got it. I got it."

He then tried to release himself from their tight hugs and said, "I sensed you'd need help but didn't know you'd face Nargorg."

"If Raionar's temple is immune to any magic, including Portones, where are we now?" Baldor asked.

"I see; besides your ability to give people a heart attack, you can ask relevant questions. That's impressive," Booch answered.

Tahona and Astiak started laughing. Baldor whispered, "I said I'm sorry."

"I dug underground and came here to the Armashasb dungeons. Then I opened a Portone to see if you're somewhere near Shajar'atash. I was lucky you were there." Booch continued.

"No, we were lucky," Astiak responded.
Booch immediately said, "All right, enough, guys. I helped you because I want this planet to survive and besides, you guys are cool."

He paused for a second and then continued, "We are still in danger. These dungeons are full of guards. They don't know you, so they'll see you as intruders."

ARAMASHASB

Astiak started looking around. He now realized that they were inside a cave. The cave was dark, and the only source of illumination was a torch that was attached to the wall. At this moment, Booch grabbed the torch from the wall and said, "We should be quiet. We will follow the path to reach Armashasb's throne."

"Why does he need guards?" asked Tahona.

"And why does this guy need dungeons?" Baldor asked.
"You humans ask a lot of questions. I'll tell you once we are out of here. Just be quiet and follow my lead." Booch quietly replied.
Booch then started walking ahead and the Aeluminars began following him. He was taking each step cautiously. After walking for a few minutes in those tunnels, which looked like an infinite maze, they reached a junction where the road was divided into four. Booch stopped walking. He then started sniffing the air before saying, "Something doesn't smell right."

"What do you smell? asked Tahona."
"Something that I never smelt before. There must be something wrong," Booch responded.

"How come?" Astiak asked.
"These tunnels should be flooded with Aramashasb soldiers. We haven't seen a single guard until now," Booch replied.

After passing through many tunnels, they came to an open gate. That part of the tunnel seemed muchtaller. It was maybe 5 or

6 metres high. The gate was made of gold. On the left side of the gate, figures of horsemen running towards each other were carved. On the upper part of the gate, the image of a peacock-like creature was carved. The right side of the door was covered with words in Altomanos. They could hear the sad and beautiful sound of the harp coming from inside. After looking at the gate, the warriors looked inside. The darkness coiled inside that place. The sole gleam of light was shining through a lay light on the ceiling.

They could see two shadows. A very tall figure was caressing a horse-like creature with his right hand while sitting on his throne. Suddenly, the beautiful sound of the harp stopped. They looked to the left side of the hall and saw a girl playing the harp. The man stood from his throne and started walking towards the Aeluminars. When he came forward and stood under the spotlight, his appearance became visible. His height reached 4 metres. His face was something between a human and a goat. His eyes were black as night and his lips were dry and colourless. His beard was long and dishevelled and covered his long neck. His body was hidden under a brown hemp robe. His robe covered his arms up to his elbows and his legs below his knees. In his left hand, he had a long black wooden staff. On his neck was a green talisman. What seemed strange were his arms, especially his right arm, which was strangely thin and bony, and there were many scorches from which a black liquid like tar was coming out. His goat-like neck was covered with big warts.
The horse-like creature on his right side was the size of a full-grown horse and had a head like a viper with two stag's horns. The creature's body was covered with scales and a silver-coloured mane covered his head and neck. His snake-like eyes were like two balls of red fire. When he breathed, something like smoke came out of his nostrils.

Booch opened his mouth and asked with surprise and sadness, "What has happened to you, Lord Aramashasb, master of nature, ruler of catastrophe?"

"Who art thou?" Aramashasb whispered.
"It's me, Booch, the gardener. I serve Lord Raionar, your brother. Do you remember me?" answered Booch.

Aramashasb responded, "I have no brother, feeble creature."
He then turned his head to the Aeluminars and whispered, "Uh, three fools pursuing nothingness. You'll meet your end here. Your flesh will be devoured by Araginos. Misery will be upon those whom you love."

"Your brother, Lord Raionar, sent us here to you. He said you would let us cross the Nefarious Marshes." Baldor said.

"I have no brother and have no loyalty but to Shak'zadurath!" Aramashasb angrily responded.

Booch, with a respectful tone, asked, "So now you are allegiant to who abducted Raionar's wife?"

"Sacrifices must be made, and blood shall spill for the greater purpose," responded Aramashasb.

"Do you betray your kin for a greater purpose?"
Booch then quietly whispered, "He is a shadow of who he was."
"Silence! Prepare to face your doomed destiny. Araginos, kill these foul creatures!" Aramashasb shouted.

Araginos opened his mouth, showed his crocodile-like teeth and charged towards Astiak.
Astiak dodged his charge agilely and hit Araginos with his staff. Araginos slipped on the smooth and polished surface of the hall and a second later, he was ready to attack again. He then jumped and landed on Astiak, nailed him to the ground with his hooves, and tried to tear him to pieces with his jaws.

Astiak managed to put his staff in Araginos' mouth while holding it with both hands. Tahona dragged her dagger and started stabbing Araginos in the back. Araginos howled like a wolf and opened his jaws, which were locked on Astiak's staff, and charged towards Tahona, but in the middle of the way, Baldor, with a swift and stormy swing, brought his sword down on Araginos neck and severed his neck from his body.

Aramashasb, who was enraged by the death of Araginos, roared and threw his cloak to the ground and his body became visible to the warriors. His body was covered with obscene scorches and a black, viscous liquid. A bitter and disgusting smell filled the hall. There were four more arms hidden under his cloak, which were shorter and thinner.

"He has Raionar's curse on him," Booch whispered.

"What does it do?" asked Baldor.

"Raionar cursed Zaloth and anyone who would follow him. The curse affected Aramashasb's body and mind," Booch responded.

Aramashasb bellowed loudly, jumped high in the air and landed right where the warriors and Booch were standing. A second before that, Aeluminars dodged and flipped to evade Aramashasb's attack. Booch quickly went to take cover behind the hall door. Astiak stormed with his staff and landed a heavy attack on Aramashasb, but he easily parried Astiak's attack with his staff and hit Astiak back with a powerful swing of his staff, which threw him metres away. Baldor used this opportunity to land his flame sword on Aramashasb's right arm. The rotten arm fell to the ground and the foul, dark blood kept coming out of where it was amputated. Aramashasb growled in pain and turned his head towards Baldor. Baldor swung his sword again, but Aramashasb was ready for it.

"Khazud Otar!" whispered Aramashasb.

A meteorite-like stone came out of his staff, hit Baldor in the chest and threw him forcefully against the wall. Tahona rushed to Aramashasb with a scream and stuck her dagger in his back. Aramashasb turned around, grabbed Tahona with his four arms and struck her with a heavy forehead strike. Tahona became unconscious. He then threw her away from his arm. Tahona's body fell on the marble floor of the hall. Astiak, furious at what happened to his fellows, stood on his feet, and shouted, "Ekhno Zoha!"

A fierce dragon-shaped fireball emanated from Astiak's staff, hitting Aramashasb in the face. He screamed in pain while the fire burned through his skin. Astiak immediately cast another fire spell, but this time Aramashasb swung his staff in the air and shattered the fireball spell. He then stomped on the ground with his hoof, which caused a small earthquake around Astiak and knocked him to the ground.

Armashasb commenced walking towards Astiak to finish him. Failure was imminent.

"Feeble creatures, puppets of Mawu, your short story will end here and your kind will vanish from Dalanar after Shak'zadurath's victory. The war will eradicate anyone who stands against him," said Aramashasb.

"You must kill me first!" Baldor said this while trying to stand on his feet.

Aramashasb turned around and saw Baldor barely standing on his feet while holding his sword.

Aramashasb was ready to finish Baldor. Baldor, for the last time, looked at Tahona and was prepared to die. With the little strength left in him, he raised his sword with both hands. Aramashasb raised his wand and was prepared to cast the final spell on him, but suddenly, Astiak, with all his power, shouted, "Qot Mohirog!"

The spell hit Aramashasb and nailed him to the ground. This time, his spell was so powerful that Aramashasb could not get rid of the thorns that tangled all over his body.

Booch, who was observant until that moment, whispered to himself, "Forgive me, my lord, we must stop your brother."
He then charged towards Armashasb, jumped on his hexed body, took Zaloth's talisman from his neck and threw it on the ground.

Baldor started hobbling towards Aramashasb. He was holding the grip of his sword with his hand and dragging the blade on the ground.
We came in peace. All we wanted was to pass from here, but you killed Tahona. You deserve to die.

Aramashasb broke the hex with the remaining of his power, grabbed Booch, who was standing in front of him, from his coat, brought him in front of his face, and shouted, "You foul little mouse, you've taken my talisman from me. You shall… "

Before finishing his sentence, Baldor put his sword in Aramashasb's stomach. Aramashasb released Booch and, with a loud howl, fell to the ground.

The lord of catastrophe had fallen.

Baldor let the sword fall from his hand and, while limping, started to walk towards Tahona. Astiak walked towards Booch and, when he reached him, found out about the sadness in his eyes.

"I betrayed my lord. I killed Aramashasb, Lord Raionar's brother. He will never forgive me," said Booch.
Astiak kneeled and, with an assuring tone, said, "You had done nothing wrong. You didn't betray Lord Raionar. That creature was no more Aramashasb; he was up to no good. You saved our lives twice."

Astiak then looked at the talisman of Zaloth and said, "That talisman consumed all good in Aramashasb. I still wonder why he turned his back to his brother and bound with Zaloth."

Baldor reached Tahona. He kneeled, grabbed her left hand and said, "You're still alive."

While breathing heavily, Tahona, with eyes shut, said, "I will not die before throwing you inside a waterfall."

A tiny teardrop ran down Baldor's cheek. He laughed and said, "I'll be waiting for that."

He then continued, "Do you think you can stand up on your feet?"

"Yes, I just have a terrible headache. A painkiller would work," said Tahona.

Baldor helped Tahona stand up and said, "I'll call the pharmacy, so consider it done."
"Haha, very funny," said Tahona. They then walked towards Astiak and Booch.
Astiak and Booch turned their faces towards Tahona and Baldor. Astiak said, "You guys look terrible."
Baldor responded, "We didn't have time to take a bath."

Astiak smirked and said, "You need to go to a carwash. A bath only won't work on you."
"And you definitely need a barber," said Tahona.

"Haha, now you don't feel the pain anymore, right?" Baldor wondered.

Tahona smiled and said, "Making fun of you makes me feel better."

"All right, I can handle that," said Baldor.

Booch, still upset, said, "Thank you for saving me, Baldor."

"This was the first nice thing you said about me," Baldor noted this and went closer to Booch, kneeled, and continued, "we thank you for saving us twice in one day. We appreciate what you did, and that beast was an enemy to us, you and Raionar. Don't feel guilty about it."

At this moment, the harpist girl said, "O'Aeluminars!'

Everyone had forgotten about her at that moment. They turned around to see her again.

"You shall open the gate to the Nefarious Marshes with the Elder Staff."

"Who are you?" asked Astiak.

"She is Lady Alena, daughter of Aramashasb and Dena," Booch responded.

"Why are you telling us this? We… just killed your father," wondered Tahona.

Alena responded, "The fallen man was merely a shadow of who he was. My father died long ago when he sought help from the lord of deceit."

"Why did he seek help from the worst being in existence?" asked Baldor.

"Despair made him do what he did. My mother, Dena, was killed by Nargorg, Zaloth's servant. He became deeply sorrowful. He forgot himself and was lost in his memories of my mother. He forgot that he had a daughter until Zaloth came. He promised my father that he'd be able to see my mother again only if he made a loyalty pact with him. I warned him of Zaloth, but it was too late. My father wanted to see his wife again and nothing could stop him," Alena answered.

Alena put her head down and continued, "The vow was made and Zaloth gave him the cursed talisman. That was the day my father died. He became Zaloth's puppet, didn't eat, didn't think and only obeyed his orders."

"Did he bring back your mother?" Tahona asked.

"Death is final, just like for your kind. Unless Mawu or Ahrima decide otherwise," Alena remarked.

"So he tricked your father with a lie?" asked Baldor.

"He cast a mute illusion of her. My father was happy with that, but his mind and body became corrupted. He brought two curses upon himself: Raionar's and Zaloth's. He started obeying the commands of Zaloth and sent all his guards to fight for him. All I could do was sit here, play the harp and hope he remembered who he was, but I failed." Alena said sadly.

Tahona went closer to Alena, held her and said, "You didn't fail; he was long gone before all this, as you said. Your love kept you here and you did what you could. This was out of your hand."

"Thank you, Tahona"

Astiak asked, "What are you going to do now?"
"I should reach my uncle, Raionar, in haste. He should become aware of Shak'zadurath's plan," Alena answered.
Baldor asked, "Which is?"
"He wants to reign on Belanor and for that, he wants to kill the last Elohim, Melektav, and her fellowship, and this will be just the beginning. Uncle Raionar knows that a war will be unleashed upon us soon, but he is not aware that Zaloth is gathering allies and preparing an undefeatable army, including my father's servants," commented Alena.

"What do you mean?" asked Astiak.

"He will then slowly kill every living being in your realm, but not before making it a living hell."

"Please bear with me; I'm a bit confused. So, if we fail to find Melektav, the entire planet will be destroyed; this is what happened to the others who tried and failed before us. This is what the Haruns told us. Now, if Zaloth kills Melektav, he'll torture and kill everyone on Earth." Baldor stated, looking confused.

"What you know is true, but many things have changed. Zaloth wants to have Earth as his own kingdom, and he has the blessing of Ahrima. Mawu is adornment now; the only thing between him and his desire is Melektav. You must protect Melektav by all means; otherwise, the reign of Zaloth will begin. You have to go now and pass through the Nefarious Marshes. You should not waste a second. I will go to my uncle," Alena then stood up and said, "Blessing of Mawu be upon you, Aeluminars. The destiny of this planet is in your hands."

Booch, without hesitation, said, "I'll come with you, milady. I have to say what I did and face what I should face."

Alena bent over, touched Booch's face with her hands and said, "You've done what you must've done, my dear Booch. Leave this part for me and worry not. Your friends need you. You should guide and protect them."

"Thank you, my lady," Booch said.

"We thank you, Booch; you saved us from what devoured my father. Now go."
Alena whispered a spell and opened a portone. She then turned to the Aeluminars and said, "Farewell, warriors."
She walked inside the portal and after a second, the portal vanished.

Baldor walked towards where the staff was, kneeled and grabbed it from the ground. The staff was 1 ½ metres long and made of black wood. The surface of the staff was smooth and polished, and a dark green pearl was placed in the handle. Baldor then walked towards the stone-made door behind Aramashasb's throne. He tried to find a clue where he could use the staff, but he didn't find anything. He then said disappointedly, "She said we need to use it to open the door, but how?"

Tahona and Astiak walked towards the door and started searching.
"You need to place it inside this hole," Booch said while pointing to a small hole in the ground.
Baldor placed the staff in the hole and said with a smile, "And you wanted to leave us."
The stone gate started opening with loud rumbles. It took several seconds before the gate was completely opened. In front of them, they saw a cave lit by the light of the torches installed on the walls. The dirt ground outside the gate continued for 20 metres and at the end, it led to the marsh. A small wooden raft was waiting for them to continue their journey.

BELANOR
SIOPILOS
NAMALMÛR
RAJONAR
BARAHUT
NEFARIOUS
SHAJAR'ATASH
ARAMASHASB
SHAJAR'ANAK
N
BARDUK

BOOK CREDITS

Editor: Helen Muriithi

Cover book designer: Stefan Raczkowski

Map editor: Z Sajjad

Printed in Great Britain
by Amazon